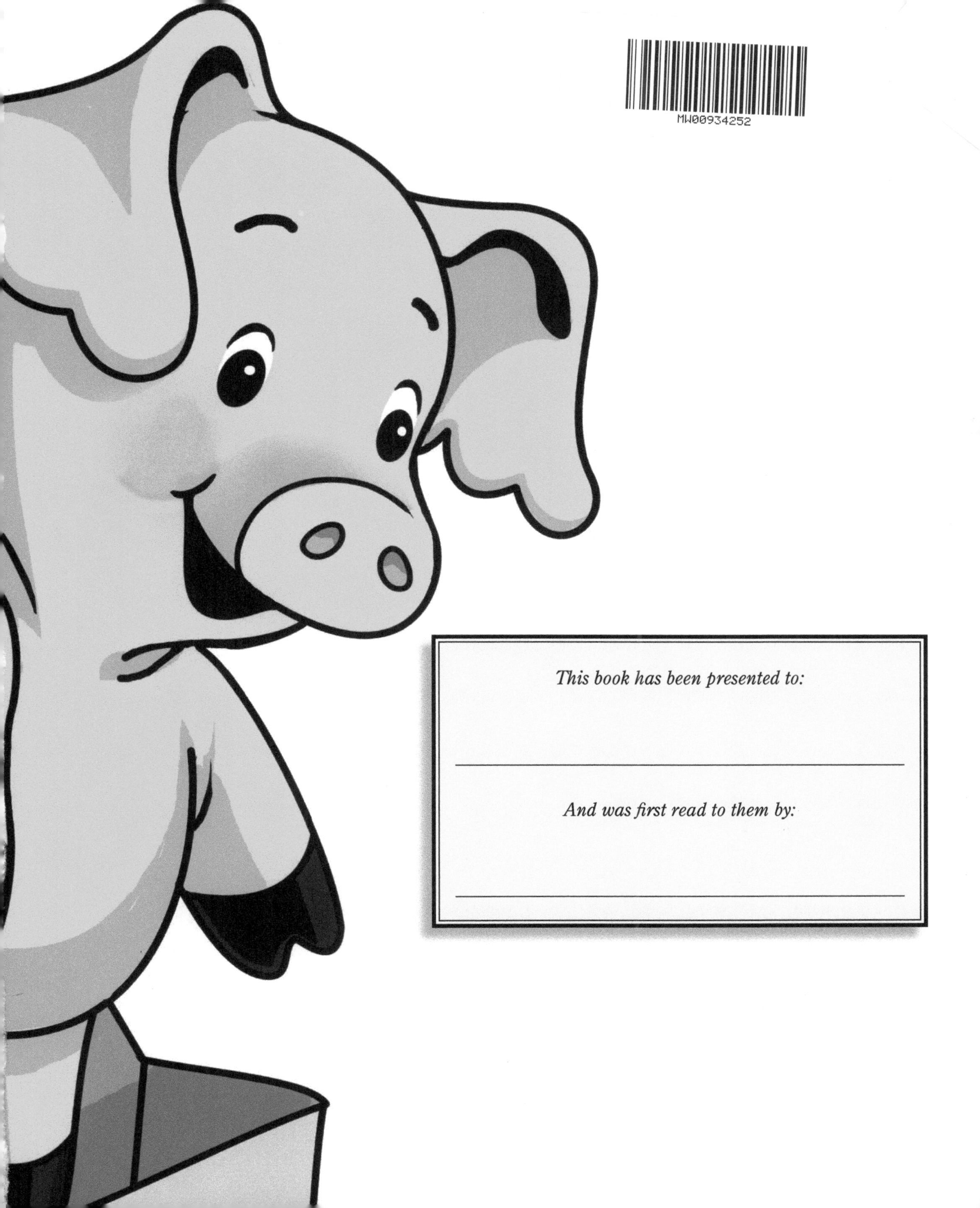
MW00934252
This book has been presented to:
And was first read to them by:

The Reading Pig Goes To New York City

Author—Susan Shinn, Ed.D.

Illustrator—Judy Nostrant

Foreword—Michael Schwanenberger Ed.D.

Teachers Change Brains Media books may be purchased for educational, business or sales promotional use.
For information – www.thereadingpig.com
Library of Congress Cataloging in Publication Data is available on request.

ISBN – 9781736988909 First edition. April, 2021

Book management & marketing services – www.maxfemurmedia.com

Illustrations – Judy Nostrant

Book layout and production — Pattie Copenhaver

Acknowledgements ~

The Reading Pig's adventures continue because of the contributions of the following teachers, partners and generous donors.

Emily Meschter, DHL – In 2012, Emily Meschter was awarded an Honorary Doctor of Humane Letters degree by the University of Arizona, College of Education for her long and distinguished career as a philanthropist and supporter of education. In 2010, the Flowing Wells Unified School District honored Emily for her incredible contributions to the district by creating the Emily Meschter Early Learning Center. Emily's support of the Reading Pig Goes to New York City is another example of her extraordinary service to education. Emily Meschter has provided major funding which provides free copies of The Reading Pig Goes to New York City to students.

Sara Piekarski – is a Speech Language Pathologist at the Emily Meschter Early Learning Center and was a major contributor to The Reading Pig Goes to New York City.

Jessica Jankowski-Gallo – is a General Education Teacher at the Emily Meschter Early Learning Center. In addition to being a major contributor to The Reading Pig Goes to New York City, Jessica was the lead author of The Reading Pig Goes to the Desert.

Jennifer Anglin, Editor – Jennifer is an invaluable member of the publishing team. Her editing skills are incredible and help The Reading Pig series model effective writing skills for future young authors.

Judy Nostrant – As the Reading Pig series Illustrator, Judy continues to amaze by capturing the spirit of reading in pictures.

Pattie Copenhaver – As the Reading Pig series Graphic Designer, Pattie brings the entire book to life.

Tim Derrig – As the Reading Pig series Book Manager, Tim handles all the details, big, small and everything in-between.

Dean Ramona Mellott – Dean Ramona Mellott is the Dean of the Northern Arizona University College of Education. Dean Mellott was instrumental in securing an NAU Eminent Scholar Grant which provided the funds needed to publish The Reading Pig Goes to New York City and additional funds to provide copies of the book to schools.

Dr. Michael Schwanenberger – Dr. Schwanenberger is a former Superintendent of Schools and the current Department Chair in Educational Leadership at Northern Arizona University. Dr. Schwanenberger penned the introduction to The Reading Pig Goes to New York City.

Nancy Serenbetz – Nancy Serenbetz is the Development Officer at Northern Arizona University. Nancy supports all the Ernest W. McFarland Citizen's Chair in Education activities including The Reading Pig Early Childhood Literacy Project.

Desert Lab Studio – As a corporate partner, Desert Lab Studio created and maintains The Reading Pig series website. www.thereadingpig.com

My gratitude, Nic

This book is dedicated
to Dr. Rene' Ground
who has been an
inspiration during my
many years in
Education. She has
been patient with
my continued
learning,
unwavering in her
devotion to my many
new concepts
and ideas, but
mostly...
forever a friend.

ISBN: 9781736988909
Published by:
Teachers Change Brains Media

www.legendaryteacher.com

A special foreword

Michael Schwanenberger Ed.D.

Dr. Sue Shinn-Olson has taken The Reading Pig on another exciting adventure. Northern Arizona University's Department of Educational Leadership and I are thrilled that we are able to financially support The Reading Pig Series latest publication, through the Arizona Board of Regents –Eminent Scholar funds, and as a university leader I am delighted to support the development of READERS, from pre-kindergarten through university doctoral degrees.

The importance of reading in the lives of children has been well documented. The development of reading skills, at the earliest possible age, is the key to future learning, and it is the strongest predictor of success in school. As the technological advancements in society entice us beyond our wildest imagination, there will always be place for a good book. Books allow, and encourage us to communicate verbally, share our stories with each other and experience the world together, not in isolation. "The Reading Pig Goes to New York City," begins with Emily, a recent transplant to the desert, from over 3000 miles away, New York City. Through the book, Emily's class and her newly found friends, are able to take a field trip to one of the largest cities in the world, New York City. Of an even greater distance than the mileage, are the differences which the students experience: the sights, the sounds, the smells, the people, the cultures and the unforgettable monuments, landmarks and historical centers. Places and things most children are only able to read about.

Thank you Dr. Shinn-Olson and Dr. Clement for inspiring us to read through the publication of another Reading Pig story. There will always be a place for a good book. Enjoy your experience and keep reading!!!

Dr. Michael Schwanenberger
Department Chair-Educational Leadership
Northern Arizona University
College of Education

Enjoy the tale...

Hi, my name is Amanda.
I want to tell you about an exciting adventure.

It was Emily's turn for show and tell. Emily was new to our class. Emily looked puzzled. Why was Cole holding a pig?

We introduced the Reading Pig to Emily. We explained that Dr. C gave our class the Reading Pig to encourage us to read and share our stories.

Emily smiled and shared her story. She had just moved from New York City. Emily told us that New York City was very different compared to Arizona.

Different sights, different sounds, and different smells. She loved New York City and was sad to leave.

CENTRAL PARK
GREAT LAWN
SHAKESPEARE'S GARDEN
BELVEDERE CASTLE
THE LAKE
BOW BRIDGE
SHEEP MEADOW
ZOO TICKETS →
ZOO ENTRANCE →
DOWNTOWN LOOP
STATUE OF LIBERTY
Sightseeing
TAXI
TAXI
HOT DOG

Cole raised the Reading Pig above his head. Our teacher, Miss Sue, knew that Cole wanted to ask a question. “Can we visit New York City on a field trip? Emily can be our guide.”

Miss Sue thought that was a great idea. She asked Dr. C and he said yes! He then asked if he could come along. He had never visited New York City. Emily was thrilled. We were thrilled. The Reading Pig was thrilled to go on another adventure.

Miss Sue asked Emily to help plan our trip. Emily said we should visit her favorite places. Miss Sue wrote the names of these places on cards. We each picked one and pinned it on the "Places We Want to Visit in New York City board".

I picked the Statue of Liberty. Cole picked Central Park. Dr. C picked the Empire State Building. The Reading Pig picked the American Museum of Natural History.

Places We Want
in New York City
CENTRAL PARK
EMPIRE
BUILDING
STATUE OF LIBERTY
AMERICAN MUSEUM OF NATURAL HISTORY

Most of us had never been on an airplane. Miss Sue, Dr. C and the flight attendants helped us put our travel bags in the cubbies above our seats. We even got a pin shaped like airplane wings.

The nice flight attendant told us it is just like the pin that the captain wears on his uniform.

Cole asked “What is a captain?” Miss Sue said the captain flies the airplane.

We fastened our seatbelts and heard a *knock knock* sound coming from the cubbie over Dr. C's head. Dr. C asked the flight attendant to open the cubbie. Guess who was making the *knock knock* sound?

You were right. It was our friend the Reading Pig. He wanted to sit with us and help us read our favorite book during our trip.

I buckled the Reading Pig up and roar went the airplane's jet engines. The huge plane took off. We all shouted "New York City here we come!"

Our first stop was the Statue of Liberty. We traveled in a big red double-decker bus through New York City. Guess who wanted to sit on top? Right again. Emily took the Reading Pig to the top and we followed. We had a great view of the sight and sounds of the big city: cars honking, construction jackhammers pounding, helicopters whapping and ambulance sirens screeching.

The Statue of Liberty
was standing tall
and proud. Emily
shared that the
Statue of Liberty
was about 306 feet
tall. I wondered why
the Statue of Liberty
looked green.
Miss Sue said it is
covered in copper
and copper turns
light green from
the weather.

Our next stop was Central Park. Emily said she loved visiting Central Park with her family because it was so big and there were so many things to do. The Reading Pig helped us read the sign. Statues, gardens, a bridge, a castle, fountains and a zoo. We all shouted, "We want to go to the zoo!"

The Reading Pig looked afraid. We told him we would not leave him at the zoo.

CENTRAL PARK
GREAT LAWN
SHAKESPEARE'S GARDEN
BELVEDERE CASTLE
THE LAKE
BOW BRIDGE
SHEEP MEADOW
CAROUSEL
FOUNTAINS
PLAYGROUND
ZOO
THE POND
ZOO TICKETS →
ZOO ENTRANCE →

The Central Park Zoo had lots of animals. Emily told us that some of the animals were endangered. The Red Pandas were our favorite!

We saw Tamarin Monkeys.
We saw Thick Billed Parrots.
We saw Wyoming Toads.
We saw Grizzly Bears.

The Reading Pig was happy to be back in his seat on the red double-decker bus. We were on our way to the next stop, Dr. C's pick: The Empire State Building!

The red double-decker bus stopped at a stoplight. We could smell lots of different foods. Hot dogs, pretzels, nuts and pizza were being cooked in carts. The smells were wonderful and made us very hungry.

We got off the bus. Miss Sue and Dr. C helped us buy our favorite food to eat. My hot dog had lots of mustard and I got a bright red frozen drink. Mmmmm Good!

mmmmm!
HOT DOG

We looked up in awe at the beautiful Empire State Building. I asked Dr. C how tall was the Empire State Building. He said it was 1,454 feet tall. Cole asked how tall was the Reading Pig. Dr. C said about 1 foot. We were amazed!

Emily said we could take an elevator up near the top of the Empire State Building. We went up and could see for miles. People below looked like ants. We were astounded!

The red double-decker bus took us to the American Museum of Natural History. We visited a cool exhibit about volcanoes. We could see and hear the fiery eruption. Cole put his hands over the Reading Pig's ears.

Next we visited a butterfly exhibit. We were able to walk among butterflies we had never seen. I saw two butterflies that were very colorful. One was green and one was blue. The Reading Pig helped me read a sign about butterflies. The blue one was named a blue morpho and the green one was a green birdwing. I am going to find out more about them when I get back to school.

Blue
Morpho
Green
Birdwing

Emily took us to her favorite exhibit. We were surprised to see a huge skeleton of a Tyrannosaurus Rex. We all looked up in admiration for this magnificent creature!

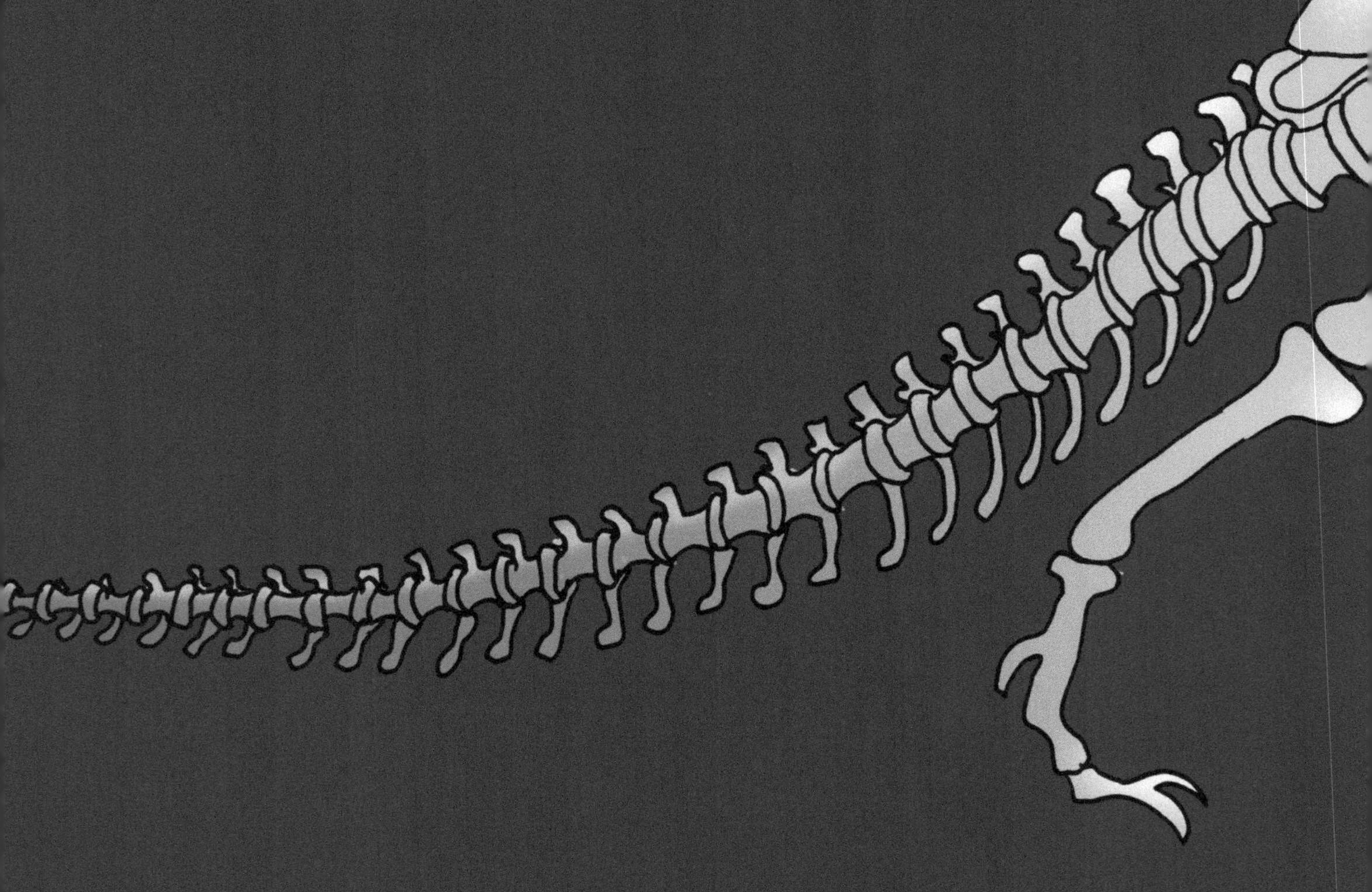

The big red double-decker bus took us to our hotel to sleep. The next day we packed our bags and lined up to get back on the big red double-decker bus. Emily was the line leader and I was the caboose. We were excited to go home and share our adventure with our parents. Miss Sue said we should all take a picture in front of our big red double-decker bus.

Cole shouted

"Where is the Reading Pig?"

Dr. C looked very worried and exclaimed "Oh no! This happened before. We can't leave the Reading Pig in New York City! He will get lost in this big city."

Emily whispered "What did you do to find the Reading Pig last time?" I told her we yelled *oink* three times.

We looked up and saw the Reading Pig peeking over the side of the big red double-decker bus. He already found his favorite seat on the top level of the bus. He was in the perfect spot for our picture.

We rode to the airport and had one last chance to take in the unique sights, sounds and smells of New York City. We will never forget our New York City adventure.